JUSTICE IN BLOOD

BY

Daryl McAusland

Daryl McAusland © 2024

All of the incidents that occur within this story are real life incidents that were attended and dealt with by the author. The Author was a serving police officer and has extensive experience in dealing with Sexual offences, Counter terrorism, firearms and Custody.

Names, locations have all been changed to protect the identity of all the parties involved.

This is a blend of fact and fiction, the aftermath of the incidents are not real and no suspects written about within the story were actually harmed.

Daryl McAusland © 2024

This uses inspiration from real cases and they are of a graphic nature so readers discretion is advised.

Daryl McAusland © 2024

CHAPTER 1–

Clerk: "All rise"

Judge: "Foreman has the jury arrived at a unanimous decision?"

Foreman: "Yes"

Judge: "For the murder of Gary Parsons how find the Jury guilty or not guilty?"

Foreman: "Guilty"

Judge: "For the murder of Liam Howard how find the Jury guilty or not guilty?"

Foreman: "Guilty"

Daryl McAusland © 2024

Judge: "For the murder of Ian Sutherland how find the Jury guilty or not guilty?"

Foreman: "Guilty"

Judge: "For the murder of Patrick Mahoney how find the Jury guilty or not guilty?"

Foreman: "Guilty"

Judge: "For the murder of Robert Hall how find the Jury guilty or not guilty?"

Foreman: "Guilty"

Judge: "For the murder of Neil Doherty how find the Jury guilty or not guilty?"

Foreman: "Guilty"

Judge: "For the murder of George Lee how find the Jury guilty or not guilty?"

Daryl McAusland © 2024

Foreman: "Guilty"

Judge: "For the murder of Kayleigh Barns how find the Jury guilty or not guilty?"

Foreman: "Guilty"

Judge: "For the murder of Jamie Andrews how find the Jury guilty or not guilty?"

Foreman: "Guilty"

Judge: "For the murder of James Baker how find the Jury guilty or not guilty?"

Foreman: "Guilty"

Judge: "Mr. Morgan please rise, after a long-drawn-out trial, you have been found guilty of murder on all ten counts.

Ohhhhh shit, ok things haven't gone to plan, so let me introduce myself now we have gone through all the boring stuff, I am Jack Morgan I was a police officer, yes was as now after this I'm a convicted criminal. Here I am sat in the dock of the crown court, wearing my best suit in an attempt to not like some common criminal. This case had generated quite a lot of media attention and so I am sat here being looked upon from a packed gallery, family members of the victims, members of the press all glaring at me. It feels as if their stares are burning into my very soul. Not a nice place to be, I can tell that a lot of the people here are after my blood, but luckily, I am protected by the same system that helps protect criminals that really don't deserve to live. My family have given up on me, my actions have caused my own family to disown me and so as with birth you come into this world alone and it would appear I am going out the same way.

Daryl McAusland © 2024

I wasn't always like this; I once followed the letter of the law. Problem is the law is an arse and unfortunately the red tape wrapped around procedures and the unrelenting fight against the crown prosecution service means putting bag guys in prison is a near impossible task and they walk among us, when their breathing is a crime against the victims they've left behind. In the current day I will probably be seen as a villain, a murderer a vigilante but I will let history be my true judge, I will let my deeds be seen for what they truly are and will be remembered as a hero. Willing to do what others daren't to make our streets and homes a safer place. So, you are right in thinking I have no remorse, I did what I did and would do it again, when you hear what these people and I say people loosely did you too will arrive at the same conclusion, they voided their right to exist.

Daryl McAusland © 2024

But back to my fate, prison, locked away from the world. Which I feel is a waste, I had so much more to give and more people to save.

Judge: "Mr Morgan, for the murders of ten people and with no remorse or shred of regret I am going to sentence you with the full power of this court, you are sentenced to whole life imprisonment, Mr Morgan, the level of brutality and wickedness you have shown, the abuse of power and authority and the damage you have caused to public confidence in trusting the police means that life means life, you will never be free to take up the freedoms of this country. Bailiffs take him down."

With this the court erupted, people in the gallery cheering, the judge calling for order, lots of shouting towards me, hard to make out but I got the general vibe, I was hated and they wanted my blood. As an ex-police officer I can tell you that the fellow inmates where I would be residing also felt the same, I knew this before they even got to know what I had done, simply because a dirty cop instantly has a target on their backs.

Well, if I'm being honest, I'm not surprised, angry yes, surprised no. I am angry that I am being punished for doing what the police could not and would not do, the number of lives I have saved due to my actions outweigh my deeds. Well let me start at the beginning and let you decide if I'm good or bad? I am being honest I have done everything I'm being accused of, but what is always missing is the context, the why, the reason a law-abiding good police officer decides to blur the lines.

So, if you continue on this path, please be aware this isn't pretty, I'm not going to hold my punches and this ride gets bumpy.

So, let's begin...

Daryl McAusland © 2024

[CHAPTER 2] —

You're still here? Well, if you are sure, let me tell you where I began, where I came from and maybe give you some insight into my mind.

That's all everyone seems to be interested in? What drives someone to kill, the thoughts and views of a killer.

Well, I was born around midnight in August, late August, I'm a Virgo, now if you know anything about serial killers this star sign is quite prominent with serial killers. That's if you believe that nonsensical mumbo jumbo, I don't think it has any bearing on how I turned out, but what do you believe?

I was born in London, south east London to be precise, the home of the mighty Charlton Athletic football team. I am proud of my heritage but when I grew up, the sights, smells and general feel of London repulsed me and eventually I moved away. You see I like peace; I like order and the hustle and bustle of the big city didn't suit how I wanted to live, but I never minded working somewhere busy. You see I am a simple man and when I envisioned the future, wife, kids, house and dogs I didn't see that being in London, having grown up in London I didn't really want to rasie a family and start a life somewhere like this.

I was taken home from the hospital with my mother and father and I was their first-born child. My parents were extremely young, my mother only just old enough to be allowed legally to have me and my father only a few years older. I was born to two very young, very immature parents, some might say children.

Being so young and inexperienced in life their relationship was fiery and my father in particular was violent and would get jealous if I received new things and he didn't, this would escalate into arguments and arrive with my mother being physically abused. This is something to this day I hate to even think about. This continued through my early years until one day my father in a fit of rage kicked open the living room door with me behind causing me to go flying. This for my mother was her breaking point and my father was kicked out. I never saw him again, in fact I have very few memories of the early years, but knew enough in my gut that he was a piece of shit. The fact I feel so strongly that he is no good that even when I got older, I have never reached out, never cared to know him or his side of the family. Equally he has never reached out to me

Daryl McAusland © 2024

so that just adds more weight to my belief that he is scum and not worth my time.

Fast forward a few years, my mother is in a healthy new relationship and I have been taken on and raised by a man who treated me like his own and who I still to this day call my dad. The years leading up to my teens were uneventful, the trauma of my early years forgotten and I was happy. My mother was happy and was being treated how a woman should be treated in a relationship.

My fondest memories are of us as a family, going on adventures, holidays and just generally being a stable happy family. Don't get me wrong we were never rich not by a mile and I wasn't able to go on a foreign holiday until I was making my own money.

Daryl McAusland © 2024

My Dad worked two jobs so my mother could go to college and university to become a teacher, this man showed me through actions how a man should behave.

So, with such a good role model, why did I end up killing people? Well having such a good role model showed me right from wrong, when you see injustice and victims not getting what they deserve, it takes a special person to step up and do what's required.

My life away from the family home outside playing with my friends was typical, we would go out and get up to mischief, but nothing bad enough to ever get arrested. I never abused animals, I had no inclination to casue harm. I just got on with my life and tried to remain the grey man never raising my head above the parapet. Similary I was also not bullied, something you hear a lot from people when you are arresting you is "I bet you got bullied as a kid" which wasn't the case, my want to be a police officer was to good and protect people, make real change so that incidents similar to what happened to my mother wouild never be replicated again.

So pretty much my life was easy, I did well at school getting high grades and decided at an early age that helping people was going to be my calling and so joining the police at 18 was an easy decision, it was one I had dreamed of as a child. The other options on my list where Vet, firefighter and paramedic so overall I wanted my life to be one of helping people and making real change. Don't get me wrong the dream of being rich and care free was just that a dream, I came from a family that wasn't particularly well off and so was aware that my life would probably follow the same path, enough money to get by, not rich but comfortable and hopefully happy.

Daryl McAusland © 2024

The moment I was old enough I made sure my fitness was at a level where I could pass the initial tests and prepared myself for interviews and exams. Everything I passed with flying colours which opened the door to attending police college and initial training.

Here I learnt the law, police procedure and investigation techniques.

This was also where I learnt how the justice system is flawed, how guilty people can walk free and the importance of doing things procedurally by the book so cases don't get thrown out. But you don't fully appreciate just how important that is and how bad it can be until you are having to tell a victim that a case failed at court because of your incompetence.

But at this point in my life, I was happy, hardworking, healthy but naïve to the workings of the real world.

Daryl McAusland © 2024

I still at this stage had complete faith in the justice system and had upmost respect for the uniform I wore and the oath I took.

To be fair even now at this point in prison I still respect the oath and feel my actions that led me here were still in keeping with my original directive, so save life and limb.

So that was that, once I'd finished all my training, I had a passing out parade where my family and friends were able to come and celebrate me becoming a fully fledged police officer, one of my proudest moments and then I was unleashed onto the world to go and seek out injustice and crime and make things right.

I moved into my own place away from the family home, went out into the world to forge my path as an adult. I rented a flat in a quiet village location, one bedroom, living room etc the basic living accommodation I could work and live in relative peace. I had to learn to do all the adult chores on my own, cooking, cleaning and the dreaded cruel task of changing a duvet cover, I was in charge of my life and my decisions were my own.

So, no glaringly obvious psychotic clues, I didn't torture animals, I had a good male and female role model, I had your stereotypical upbringing give or take a few minor hiccups along the way.

Unless you can see something I can't? I don't think my upbringing or experiences led me to what I eventually became.

Daryl McAusland © 2024

[CHAPTER 3] –

So now you know about my backstory, who I am, my morals, my ethics. You may be wondering what changed? What caused a person who respected the law, fought for justice to change? Well, this is where it all began, this is where the punishment or lack of punishment did not fit the crime, this was where I found my true calling. Still protecting the public but working outside the lines.

So, what made me start thinking that there was an issue with the justice system, what made me start to question everything that I was taught? Like with everything there is normally a trigger point, an event that makes you question everything, well this was mine, the first chip in the armour of the justice system that I actually saw for myself and began to question if it was up to the task of truly protecting the people.

Upon joining the police, I went through the same process as every other police officer, taken out for a period of time with a more experienced officer, shown the ropes and how to catch the bad guys but also the paperwork required to make sure that when the case went through the rigmarole that is the court system it stuck.

This beginning process that you go through also shows you just how bad the systems in place actually are, how you can have the most watertight case and still the bad guys walk. Not an easy pill to swallow, the more it happens, the more your faith in the system erodes.

Daryl McAusland © 2024

So, I was outside of my probation period and it was early on in my career, I was out on patrol, normal day, nothing to prepare me for what I was about to face.

Reports came over the radio for a job which was for units to attend a car versus Lorry RTC (Road traffic Collision) I was close by so I called up on the radio and began to make my way to the scene, a car having a fight with a lorry never ends well and I was nervous to see what kind of destruction I was about to face.

I'd been to accidents before where people hadn't faired to well, so was mentally preparing myself for the worst. The problem was there is nothing that can prepare you for what I was about to deal with. The role of the emergency services is unique, you can face the worst that humanity can throw at you at lunchtime and then go and have dinner with your kids in the evening and need to act like everything is ok, pretending like you haven't just got back from hell.

So, driving as fast as I was allowed, ensuring I was safe but quick, I joined the motorway and, in the distance, I could see a column of black smoke, fuck this was bad! I've continued going and hit the back of stationary traffic, I've joined the hard shoulder and made my way towards the smoke, in the distance I could see flames and so I've immediately requested the fire service to attend, I needed to get there. I've finally arrived on scene after what felt like an eternity, I was met by a horrific site, the lorry had run into the back of the car and was on the hard shoulder of the motorway, the car had smashed into the central reservation where it remained and instantaneously burst into flames with the occupants inside. I could hear them screaming as I've tried to get close to the car to try and save them, the heat was unbearable, I could feel my skin burning, my

Daryl McAusland © 2024

uniform starting to smoulder, I was intent on saving them, it is in my blood to help people and I wasn't going to allow a few burns to stop me. I was shouting to them, asking if they could get out of the car, trying to reassure them that I was doing everything in my power to save them. I got closer before being dragged back by a firefighter who had arrived on the scene:

"LET ME GO!!!"

I screamed at them, I needed to save them, they didn't let me go and immediately other firefighters used their hoses and got water onto the car in attempt o extinguish the flames, other firefighters began to push everyone back who had got out of their cars and were watching, some filming the incident unfolding. This is something I have never understood about the human condition, why there is this morbid fascination with people's misfortune, you see it all the time at your standard car crashes with vehicles slowing down to have a good look, which has always baffled me

Daryl McAusland © 2024

and also why if you are stuck in slow moving traffic generally this is the reason as they need to get their fix. Well, these voyeurs needed to move well back for fear of the car exploding, as this was happening the water hitting the hot car was making the smoke worse and it started to bubble and pop, I could no longer hear the screams from the car. My worst fears had been realised, I was too late and they had unfortunately died from the fire, hopefully quickly through smoke inhalation, but nonetheless they were dead and I couldn't save them.

Now, the driver of the lorry had been detained and upon the arrival of specialist traffic officers he was arrested for causing death by dangerous driving. An investigation was carried out and the driver of the lorry was found to be on his phone at the time of the crash, he killed them through his stupidity and negligence and when it went to court, he was given a 10-year prison sentence. Now on the face of it

Daryl McAusland © 2024

that's a good job, tea and medals for all parties involved however what I haven't told you is that the people in the car where a mum, dad and their two children, a family gone! So, I was struggling with this prison sentence, so according to the court a human life was only worth 2.5 years? Was the prison sentence imposed on the lorry driver sufficient? In my opinion the answer that that question was and will always be a resounding No!

This was when I really started to question the justice system and if criminals were actually being punished, as far as I could see they really weren't and to be honest would the lorry driver actually serve 10 years? After time taken off for being on remand, good behaviour and the possibility of early release due to overcrowding and rehabilitation schemes I would be surprised if he served even half of that sentence. The problem is that it is all cause and effect, the prisons are overcrowded, the courts are aware of this

Daryl McAusland © 2024

problem and so other punishment methods are preferred to try and take the strain off an already over capacity prison service. Being a criminal in this age is probably the best time to do it as if you show remorse, fall on your sword and say how bad you've been but you want to change the likelihood is that you will never see the inside of a cell.

This was something that began to plague my thoughts, what if he got off? How would he then be punished? My dreams were of inventive ways to deliver justice, horrible dreams that at the times disturbed me and made me question my own morals but at this stage was only a thought a fantasy but I hadn't yet had my breaking point.

This merely set the wheels in motion for what was to come.

Don't get me wrong there were plenty of incidents that I attended and dealt with that made becoming a police officer worthwhile, gave you that good feeling deep inside and made you realise that why you had become a police officer was worthwhile and worth the sacrifices.

Two examples come to mind that still to this day fill me with a sense of warmth and pride in what I had achieved, my presence alone changed their fate and set them on a new life path, one where if I hadn't of been there it could have been a lot different.

Incident one I was on duty when reports came in that there was a male in distress and acting strangely near to the train station. I made my way to the location under response conditions, by that I used my blue lights and sirens to quickly but safely arrive on the scene. Upon arrival at the train station, I began looking around for a male that matches the description, I looked everywhere around the station and upon stepping onto the platform I found him.

Daryl McAusland © 2024

He was on the tracks; he was standing on the tracks crying uncontrollably. I immediately spoke to the make trying to get his attention and trying to persuade him to get off of the tracks. The male was so consumed with whatever that was affecting him and was ignoring my requests and my attempts to communicate had failed. Now the platform had a number of people there, they were watching the unfolding scene and I was very aware that if he was to be hit by a train that they would be witness to a horrible sight, I'd been to many incidents where people had taken on a fast-moving locomotive and they never win. I was on my own, I'd requested more help over the radio and made them aware of the developing situation. They told me that they would make contact with the British transport police and I was not to enter the tracks. Now this incident was just about to get a whole lot worse as I could see in the distance the lights of a train coming towards our location, I decided that there and then I would have to ignore what I was told on the radio as

Daryl McAusland © 2024

my main purpose as a police officer was the preservation of life and limb. So, against my better judgment I made my way down onto the tracks, I went up to the male and again spoke to him trying to persuade him to leave the tracks, again I was ignored, he was crying, holding his head and not interacting with me, this had now become time critical as there was a train approaching. I grabbed the male around his waist and hoisted him onto my shoulder in what some would call a fireman carry and walked him over to the edge of the platform. The male was protesting and screaming for me to let him die, I rolled him onto the platform and then jumped up onto the platform to join him. No more than a few seconds passed and the train was hurtling through the station at speed as it was non-stopping the station. I had the male pinned to the floor and once the train had passed, I was then able to speak and I sectioned him under section 136 of the mental health act which allows me the power to detain and take a person to a hospital for an assessment.

Daryl McAusland © 2024

More units arrived on scene and we were able to get him to the hospital.

Now the male was sectioned and given help for his failing mental health and due to my actions, he didn't die and later on found he was in crisis and the help he received allowed him to resume his life.

Another incident that has always stuck with me was when I had been asked to attend a sudden death, when people suddenly die it is the police's job to attend and check for anything that could be deemed suspicious and to file a report for the coroner and assist with getting the deceased removed to a mortuary. Upon arrival I was met by an elderly male who seemed very confused and wasn't in the best condition physically, he looked undernourished and like he wasn't wearing clean clothes. His wife had unfortunately died in her sleep and he was being looked after by her until she died, the male had no immediate family and I was worried upon removing his deceased wife and leaving the house that he wouldn't be able to look after himself and he would be a potential danger to himself. I arranged for the coroner and whilst doing this I also was making calls to social services to ensure that the husband wouldn't be abandoned.

I was able to get this man help and he was assisted by social services who took over and helped.

Many years later I had another call to the same address for a completely unrelated matter, I had forgotten about the address and so upon the door being opened was met by the same man. Instantly I recognised him and he looked good, he was well fed, clean and very talkative. He didn't recognise me but I recognised him and this choked me up, it was again another instance where my actions and being present changed the future for someone for the better.

Daryl McAusland © 2024

These examples and many more are reasons why I loved my job, why I was doing what I was doing.

Daryl McAusland © 2024

[CHAPTER 4]

But this is where it truly began, dealing with that horrific incident watching a family burn to death in front of me, powerless to help opened my eyes and got me thinking about if the punishment fitted the crime and what I was about to go through cemented my fate. The good incidents that I had attended were being outweighed by the horrible shit jobs and this was taking its toll, almost like a set of scales the bad was really outweighing the good.

So, it was a normal day, I got into work as normal, put on my uniform and booked myself on for the day. A normal day was just that, briefing on recent crimes, receiving your car and callsigns for the day, drinking tea, checking on your workload to see if you had any outstanding enquiries and just generally responding to the radio.

I had no idea that today would be the catalyst that would cause me to start handing out real justice.

So, after briefing and doing what I needed to do I was double crewed in a police car, call sign DR58 and off I went out on patrol, radio crackling with jobs and updates for other things going on. I decided to take a drive out into the countryside, driving around the rural roads I know so well. I had worked the same area for 6 years and knew what vehicles and people where local to the area and so if I saw someone or something not familiar, I would often stop and speak with them to ascertain if they were meant to be here. This is what policing used to be about, knowing your patch, your neighbourhood knowing your face and getting information, intelligence from the locals.

Daryl McAusland © 2024

Well whilst driving down one of my local routes I passed a field of Rape in full bloom, glorious bright yellow flowers and enough pollen to kill you off if you have hay fever.

In the field on my first pass was a car parked off the road to the edge of the field. Now I had never seen this car before and so I decided to investigate. I turned the car around and parked on the entrance to the field, I instructed my colleague who I was with to go to one side and I would take the other, just standard practice to ensure if anyone was in the car who wanted to escape couldn't easily.

On approach to the car, I saw the windows were steamy and I could see silhouettes of two people in the rear seats. Instant thought was it was a couple who had decided to stop off for some X-rated fun. This was something I had found many times.

I knocked on the door to car, there was a pause and movement of the silhouettes could be seen through the steamed up windows, I knocked again and the door was

Daryl McAusland © 2024

unlocked and I opened the door to be met with a man in his 30s, I asked the man what he was up to but before I could get a response I was called by my colleague in a urgent worried tone: "You need to see this"

I looked up from the male through to my colleague who was crouching by the open door on the other side of the car. Sat next to the male was a young boy around 10-11 years old, the boy was partially dressed and looked terrified with tears rolling down his cheeks.

In my gut I knew, I knew this man was the worst of humanity but I had a job to do. You are taught that everyone has to be treated with humanity and that any actions I wanted to do could cause an issue and then he would get off on a technicality, this man deserved to rot in prison, forever branded as the animal he was.

Inside I was screaming, the part of me that eventually would surface was clawing away at my conscience, the murderous rage bubbling deep inside.

Daryl McAusland © 2024

So politely I spoke to the male and arrested him on suspicion of sexual assault on a minor.

This man was then taken to custody where he was booked in with the custody sergeant and left in a cell whilst I collected evidence.

This meant having to inform the parents, watching the father of the child break down as he couldn't comprehend what had happened to his child and the internal torment of wanting to deliver his own punishment. Listening to a blow-by-blow account of the actions that happened in the car from the boy's perspective, watching his mother listening to the events and trying to keep her composure whilst internally she was screaming. Seizing all the boys clothing and escorting him to a specialist doctor for DNA and forensic photos and collection, the whole time a child, a young boy going through hell for what? The actions of that man ingrained on that child for years to come, affecting his life for years to come.

Daryl McAusland © 2024

That child went through hell for hours going through all the police processes whilst the suspect sat in his cell. Finally in the early hours of the morning everything was done, done correctly and to the best of my abilities, everything put together into an investigation report for specialist detectives to deal with in the morning, to interview and then hopefully with the blessing of the criminal prosecution service a charge to attend court. I finally after 20 plus hours of work went home, slightly haunted by the events of the night but happy in the knowledge that he would be getting dealt with and would be eventually rotting in prison, so asleep I went.

I was awoken by my phone going off next to my bed, it was late in the afternoon and I had slept for ages, on the phone was the senior investigation officer, they thanked me for all my hard work but unfortunately due to a communication on the young boys laptop and the man where the child claimed to be of legal age, the criminal prosecution service had determined there was not sufficient evidence and the male would walk free, no further action.

Now when I tell you this boy looked like a child, even if he told me he was 16 or above I would call bullshit, but no he was free to continue his predatory ways, children were still at risk, no further action? I don't think so, this was my canon event, this is what caused me to decide the police were not enough and that certain people needed to be dealt with, so I began to plan…

Daryl McAusland © 2024

[CHAPTER 5]

So, this man could not and would not get away with what he had done, the crown prosecution service may have believed his lies, but they weren't there, they didn't go through everything from start to finish, watching a family fall apart.

This made me feel sick to my stomach, I was screaming inside at how someone could do what they did and then get away with it. I thought the justice system was there to lock these people away and stop them from causing harm, not to destroy families and then get to go about their lives as if nothing had happened.

Daryl McAusland © 2024

So, step one of my plans was to cause him to be in fear and for everyone to know just what a pathetic human he was, so anonymously I leaked his details and the crime that he committed. This caused issues for him like you wouldn't believe, vigilante groups spray painting his property, posting hate mail and trying to get one on one with him. He was calling the police regularly with complaint after complaint due to level of harassment he was getting, but this in my mind was not enough, nowhere near enough to pay for what he had done. So, I decided to finish it, to make him pay.

So, over the years that I had been a police officer I learnt a lot around how the police conduct their forensics, what would get me caught and how to go about my business without the finger being pointed at me.

Daryl McAusland © 2024

Now with all the threats he was receiving it would be easy to deal with him without arising suspicion as they would pin it on them, easy win with little risk.

So, I finished work after a midday shift, it was just getting dark and was perfect to make my move. I kept my police radio with me to ensure I had an early heads-up if anything was reported and made my way to his address. I made sure prior to this through looking at previous reports in the area that there was no CCTV and that the route I took was not monitored by any ANPR cameras.

I parked a good five minutes from the address and made my way on foot keeping a low profile. Adrenaline rushing through my blood, a mixture of fear and excitement coursing through my veins, I could back out at any point but not for this, the memories of what had happened racing through my head, spurning me on.

Daryl McAusland © 2024

I was at the door; I felt sick and my leg was shaking due to the adrenaline dump. I knocked on the door, I waited awhile and nothing so I knocked again and announced through the letter box who I was. A light came on in the hall and a silhouette could be seen approaching the door through the obscured glass window. Now or never, once that door opened, I couldn't back out.

The door opens and the male instantly recognised me from our first encounter, I had preplanned this conversation so was ready: - "Evening, I have been asked to come round and discuss a strategy with you to stop the attacks on your property"

This was my way in and he invited me inside unknowing that he was very shortly going to die.

Once inside he offered me to sit and asked if I wanted a cup of tea, I agreed if he was having one as well. This was all part of my plan and he was playing his part with precision. Two teas made and placed on the coffee table, I began

Daryl McAusland © 2024

talking about different anti-social behaviour strategies and waited for my moment to accidentally spill my tea, he jumped up and said he would sort it making his way out to the kitchen leaving his tea unattended so I could drop a date rape drug into it. Having worked in the police I knew what they used, the effects and luckily where to get them.

He came back with a towel and mopped up the mess and asked if I wanted another, I declined saying I would, after we had wrapped up our business, we continued chatting and he continued drinking, this lasted around five minutes before his speech started to slur and he began to lose consciousness, perfect!

Time for action, I dragged his lifeless body onto the floor and then using different anchor points in the room tied each limb so his body was spread out like a star. I gagged his mouth so that he couldn't alert the neighbours by screaming and then I then used medical shears to cut off all of his clothes and left him there naked. To think this

Daryl McAusland © 2024

pathetic naked man had caused so much pain and misery just so he could entertain his sick twisted fantasy.

Whilst he was out of it, still unconscious I got ready, I removed any trace of my DNA by putting everything I touched into my bag and then got changed into a forensics white hooded suit, I put on a face mask and was ready for him to wake.

I sat in the chair, watching him, seemed like hours but eventually he began to stir, opening his eyes in panic, there I was in my full suit ready to deliver him the bad news.

"You seem to think you got away with what you did, well I'm here to let you know you didn't and will be punished accordingly you disgusting piece of shit"

He began violently flailing trying to free his arms, but I knew what I was doing those knots were perfect and he was not going anywhere, muffled shouts from his mouth, unable to understand what he was saying whilst his eyes darted around in panic.

Daryl McAusland © 2024

"For the sexual assault of a child I am personally sentencing you to death"

The muffled screams intensified, I didn't want to hear his bullshit excuses, the lies he told to get off the original charge, he made his choice and I made mine.

I poured petrol all over him starting at his face and down his body, making sure he was covered whilst he wriggled and squirmed trying to escape his fate, I stood over him and pulled out a match box, his eyes darted towards them in my hand, more muffled shouts, he was now bucking his body in an attempt to be free, still no avail, he was not getting away with it a second time and so I lit a match hovering it over his head, watching his eyes following the flame as if hypnotised by his impending doom and then I threw it into him, he instantly caught alight, the muffled screams intensified and I watched him contort and struggle until eventually he stopped, he was dead, the smell filling the

Daryl McAusland © 2024

room was enough to make me vomit into my suit, what the fuck had I done?

Crackle on the radio asking for units to attend a potential house fire, it was time to go as the lounge began to be engulfed in flames, time to go.

I left via the backdoor and then I garden hopped until I was in the clear. Disposing of my suit and bag of my belongings, stuffing it under a garden shed well away from house.

I made my way to my car, drove home making sure again to not trigger any cameras and to be undetected.

Once I got home, I got into the shower fully clothed, sitting on the floor, what had I just done? Yes, he deserved it, but was it my call? I was then violently sick at the thought of getting caught. I got into bed and just stared at the ceiling half expecting a knock on the door, to be punished.

Eventually I passed out and upon waking up still nothing, no phone calls, no emails and no knock on my door. I went

Daryl McAusland © 2024

online and the press article stated that there had been a murder and the police believed it was by a vigilante group. Well to say I was relieved, that's amazing! I had somehow planned and got away with murder, but I promised myself that I would let the law deal with anyone else, this was a onetime deal.

Well, we know that was bullshit and you will see why…

Daryl McAusland © 2024

[CHAPTER 6]

Back to work, now this was the true test, I was nervous as hell, half expecting to walk in and be placed in handcuffs. This was where I would know if it was game over.

So, into work I go, arrive at the police station and everyone is greeting me as normal, no funny looks, nothing? My colleague who I attended the job with came and saw me and asked me if I'd heard? Heard what? He proceeded to tell me that the guy who we arrested was dead, believed murdered by one of the vigilante groups, that CID were conducting interviews with anyone involved in the threats and hate campaign.

This was music to my ears; I had perfectly concocted the perfect storm that put them in the crosshairs. Weight was lifted and I began my day, ready to do the right thing.

CAD: 87. 999 CALL, UNITS REQUIRED TO ATTEND 36 OLD LODGE LANE, REPORTS OF A STRANGER RAPE TO A FEMALE. FEMALE ON SCENE WITH INJURIES, AMBULANCE HAS BEEN CALLED AND A SPECIALIST SEX OFFENCE TRAINED OFFICER TO BE DISPATCHED

Well funnily enough I am such an officer and had received bespoke specialist training to deal with such offences, so off I went.

I grabbed my bag with all my early evidence kit which is everything I need to fully investigate sexual offences and made my way to the scene on blue lights, incidents like this need a quick response to ensure the victim doesn't contaminate or get rid of evidence and so early steps can be put in place to identify the offender.

I arrived on scene and was met by officers who had arrived to ensure the victim was safe, the victim was a young woman, had just finished her shift as a nurse and was walking home, she stated that she was followed by a man who dragged her into bushes and beat her black and blue before sexually assaulting her. The man had pinned her down, pulled up her dress and ripped off her underwear, he then proceeded to rape her. When she was trying to fight back or call for help the man would repeatedly punch her in the face and grab her head and bang it off the floor. She eventually gave up as he was making threats to kill her, telling her this was her fault for dressing how she did and that she wanted it, kept telling her that if she didn't shut up and just take it she would not get out of this alive. This continued until the male was nearly finished and he pulled out and ejaculated all over dress before running off leaving

Daryl McAusland © 2024

her in a beaten mess on the floor of the wooded area. Now this girl was badly beaten she had cuts to her legs, arms and her face was swollen with two black eyes starting to swell, she looked like most boxers do after a full 12 rounds. I was not impressed with how a woman had been treated, not only that a nurse whose job was to help people. The whole incident gave me flashbacks to the treatment my mother used to receive and I was adamant that I would do everything to ensure if there was DNA evidence we could catch and convict the man responsible.

I did everything by the book, taking swabs, seizing clothing, accompanying her to the specialist doctor and filled out an evidential first account to ensure the facts were recorded. This was another gruelling long day, lots of internal turmoil and my past haunting me, I was livid that another human being could do this to a person.

Daryl McAusland © 2024

Once everything was completed the evidence was all booked in and a handover given to a specialist team who would work on filling in the gaps and locating a suspect. I made sure that the victim was with family and gave details of support that was available, now let's be honest, the support is a good thing but really isn't going to reverse what happened, isn't going to stop the nightmares, isn't going to make you feel safe on your own again. This crime was a crime that takes a part of a person and takes a lot of work to come out the other side nearly the same person. But I was determined to let the police do their job and the courts to lock this person away. I still had some faith in the justice system, I wanted it to work so badly as I didn't want to regress back into a killer.

This was left at that, the forensics sent off to be evaluated and I went back to my normal job.

Daryl McAusland © 2024

Few weeks passed and I was made aware that someone had been arrested for the rape, a DNA match had come back and they were interviewing the male for his suspected involvement. This was good news; this was the best news as we could do things right by the victim and justice would ultimately be served.

Well so I thought, the case was taken to court and I was asked to attend to give evidence, in the initial first account that I logged in a evidence log there was some discrepancies in what I had written and due to this their defence lawyer tore me to absolute shreds, I was made to look incompetent and stupid, now I had done everything by the book but this lawyer was doing their job to put reasonable doubt in the minds of the jury and I hated that this could be working and it was my fault.

The victim was put into the box and the questions and approach of the defence lawyer made her look terrible, he was twisting her words and making her trip up, this was not looking good.

Well, the case went on and the Jury went out for deliberation and when they came back the male was found not guilty by a jury of his peers, I watched this man celebrate as he left court and the victim breakdown, made out to be a liar and fabricating the truth.

Another kink in the justice system's armour, allowing 12 members of the public to decide, 12 people who have no legal training, 12 people who weren't there consoling a female who had been beaten within an inch of her life, 12 people who didn't promise to get her justice.

Fuck, it was once again down to me, I couldn't allow this to happen, the jury may have been turned by this male's charisma, his lies, but I for one don't give a fuck about your embellishment of the truth, I know what happened and you my friend were going to pay.

Daryl McAusland © 2024

Not only the suspect but I decided the lawyer needed to have some justice, now I didn't think he deserved to die but he needed to be punished for what he did, how can you reasonably defend a rapist, woman beating, vile piece of shit? Then get paid and extortionate amount of money and still sleep well at night? This was always something that plagued me and still to this day I cannot get my head around how money can replace someone's morals and human decency.

I was enraged and people like this was why I had joined the Police force, I joined to stop them, to keep people safe and that's exactly what I was going to do.

Daryl McAusland © 2024

[CHAPTER 7]

Time to become a serial killer, time to tread where others feared. I know I said I wouldn't kill again but this was someone walking our streets, breathing our air and a threat to our women. If a dog was to attack a human there wouldn't be a second thought, the dog would be put down for being dangerous, why should this man be any different?

Time to plan, I got his details from the crime report, researched him, where he lives and anything where he lived that could link back to me paying him a visit. I'd done this before with great success and as long as I was careful the police would never suspect a thing.

So, I managed to set up a dummy social media account and followed this excuse for a human being, turned out that he was a keen runner and would post his routes, dates etc on a regular basis, I now knew where to find him, but the how? Well, I went for a little run on the same route he takes, I dressed all in black with my hood up and scouted out any potential pitfalls and where I could get him without being disturbed. This was where I found the perfect spot, the perfect place for this person to get his punishment and for justice to be done.

So today was judgement day, I made sure that the day I did it aligned with my rostered days off to not arise suspicion. I went and hid on part of his route, knowing his routine waiting to pounce.

Daryl McAusland © 2024

I was there for a while, deep in my thoughts worried about being discovered, the thought of failure creeping in, I was going through scenarios in my head when I heard movement coming towards where I was, it was him, no time to think now. Now he had never seen me before so I was in no fear of being recognised, he ran past, I waited a second or two and then I came out and pretended as if I was on a run as well, I gained on him which wasn't hard as I'd only just started running, I got close to him in a secluded part of his route with trees either side, he had headphones on and didn't suspect a thing.

I saw my chance, I removed a handkerchief from my pocket soaked in chloroform ready for him, I jumped on his back both tumbling to the ground, I wrapped my legs around his waist and both hands round his face smothering his airway with the handkerchief, he was struggling, almost like a bucking bronco, I held on for dear life, I wasn't going to let him go so he could raise the alarm and put my life in

Daryl McAusland © 2024

jeopardy. He slowly began to tire before going motionless, luckily nobody was around and I was able to drag him by his ankles into the bushes, just like he had done. Eye for an eye he was getting the same treatment.

Now my preparation was key, I had written a suicide note for him, it stated he was really sorry for what he had done and that it had caused him to reevaluate his life and death being his only option. I wrote this with my left hand, not having some handwriting expert catching me with my pants down.

In the woods I had prepared a rope and a noose, all done with gloves to ensure I left no DNA trace. I put the rope around his neck and put the note in his pocket. I then waited with rope in hand, once he was awake, I could tell him why he had to die as I hoist him in the air.

So, I may have used to much chloroform as he was out for ages, eventually he awoke, grabbing his neck shouting what the fuck!

Well, I couldn't have him alerting everyone what was going on, so I yanked on the rope with all my strength, hoisting his body into the air. His hands grabbing at rope around his neck, kicking and thrashing, swinging in the air. I told him: -

"You may have fooled the courts, you may think you got away with what you did, you didn't, I am here to punish you for your actions and I sentence you to death, nobody will miss you and the world will be safer"

I don't know if he heard me, I don't care! He was getting what he deserved and slowly he started to stop thrashing and then he was motionless, Dead!

I didn't feel no remorse, this was what was required to keep everyone safe, this unfortunately had become my crusade

Daryl McAusland © 2024

and I was not going to let scum get away with horrible crimes.

I tied the rope off to leave him swinging and I left him there to be found, rot, pecked to pieces by birds. I honestly didn't care, fuck him, he made me do this and so I didn't care at all.

An eerie sight, just a motionless body hanging, swinging in the breeze, an offering to Mother Nature.

I quickly made my way out of the park, I had a stash bag left on my exit route, I changed my clothes and put the worn clothing into the bag and then threw them into the river.

I then made my way home, this time I wasn't feeling as panicked, I was still coming down from my adrenaline spike but felt at peace, this is what was required and so the only thing I feared was being caught, but I'd covered my bases and was confident that I was undetected.

Daryl McAusland © 2024

[CHAPTER 8]

I woke up the next day, a sudden rush of dread filling my mind as I checked my phone for anything, nothing.

So off to work I went, still nothing, but the strangest thing then happened. I was out on patrol when my call sign was called: -

"DR58, we have reports of a suicide found by a dog walker close to your location, can you attend"

What a stroke of luck, I got to go back to the scene of the crime, now the icing on the cake was that the officer attending any suicide or potential suspicious death had to determine if the incident was deemed suspicious before the body was moved to the coroner, if there were any doubts then the incidents were referred to the on-duty Inspector who then worked with specialist departments to work out if any foul play had occurred. Funnily enough I knew exactly where the suicide note was and obviously, I deemed it as a non-suspicious suicide, so off the body went to the coroner and I was in the clear once again.

This was getting too easy, the thrill of getting away with it and the feeling of doing what I deemed to be a good deed was intoxicating. I loved the fact that I was the hand of justice and I was making the scum of the earth pay in blood, but I still wasn't that far gone and still had some faith left in the justice system. Like a true addict I had convinced myself that I could quit at any time.

Now that piece of shit had been dealt with, time for the lawyer! Now like I said before, he didn't need to die, but he needed some form of punishment and nothing hurts a money-orientated snake more than doing something that hits their pocket.

I went to the court and scoped out the car park where all the court staff parked their cars, I got there nice and early before court started and waited, watching the cars pull up and park and people going to work about their day.

Then a very nice black Porsche 911 sports car turned up, parked in a space and you will never guess who gets out? That piece of shit lawyer! Now I had made up my mind that car was going to get trashed, that lawyer's pride and joy was going to take the brunt of my anger.

I checked the number plate of the car on the Police National Computer (PNC) and got the details of where the lawyer lived, I couldn't do what I wanted to do now as the car park was covered by CCTV and I wasn't getting caught for this piece of shit.

Later that night when I wasn't at work, I went out to his home address, now this man had obviously profited off the back of the misery and pain of others as this house was impressive. It was a large detached home, large wrap around driveway with an entry and exit gate, the house itself had a large glass section in the middle showing an impressive chandelier hanging over a grand staircase and wings coming off each side. This house just made me angrier as how many people had to suffer for him to achieve this opulence? Well, I wasn't prepared to kill him, but I was willing to take something he cherished and destroy it, the same way he had destroyed that girl's life. Luckily for me on the driveway was his prized possession, the beautiful black gleaming Porsche, soon to be gone. From afar I scoped out the property, I looked for any possible CCTV or alarms and then once I was happy that I could get in and out quickly with little risk of detection I made my way towards the address, I was dressed in all black and before scaling the walls I put on a balaclava to ensure I was unrecognisable. I was inside the grounds of the house, checking around constantly, the sound of a bird in a tree causing me to flinch, I was sweating profusely and felt sick with worry, but the reward was worth the risk. I got to the car and took a petrol can out of my bag and began to douse the Porsche in petrol, it was a shame as this car was so beautiful but he needed to be punished for his part. I then took out some matches, struck them and threw them onto the car, the car immediately engulfed in flames. I could feel the heat of the car on my face and it was blisteringly hot, it was time to go. I then heard a shout from towards the front of the house, it was the lawyer, he came charging towards me in pyjamas and a dressing gown, now I had the choice, fight or flight? Well, I was angry, so I chose fight and as he got nearer, I took out my police baton and smashed him straight round his face, the lights instantly went out and he slumped to the floor in a heap, I quickly checked to see if he was breathing and then fled. I ran back the way I came and made my way to my car which was

Daryl McAusland © 2024

parked a few roads away. Upon arrival at the car, I put all my clothes into a black sack and put them into a rubbish bin. Now I wanted to punish the lawyer and I felt that he had now been justly tried, his punishment wasn't death as he didn't directly do the crime but he got what he deserved. That was that and I went back to my life, work, sleep eat repeat.

So, nothing of note happened for a while, I thought that my need to kill was behind me, that my work was done, until…

CAD: 105. UNITS REQUIRED TO ATTEND REPORTS OF AN AGGRAVATED BURGLARY AT 48 LONG ACRE ROAD, VICTIMS ON SCENE WITH INJURIES, AMBULANCE HAS BEEN CALLED, NOTE ON FILE TWO VICTIMS BOTH ELDERLY

I responded on the radio and made my way on blue lights to the scene to determine what had happened and help out where I could.

Upon arrival I was met by an elderly man and woman who looked like they had gone through hell, the man had a huge swelling to his temple that looked the size of a tennis ball, blood pouring down his face and the woman was in tears her hands covered in blood wrapped up in a tea towel. I asked what had happened and it transpired that three males had broken into their house whilst they were sat down watching television, that upon bursting into the house they smashed the man round the head with a small bat knocking him unconscious. They then tied the woman to a dining room chair and started screaming where is the money, they shouted and then kicked the unconscious husband every time she said they didn't have any. When this approach failed, they pulled out a pair of pliers, they grabbed the end of her finger nails and again shouted where is the money, when this demand was again not answered the way, they wanted they systematically pulled out her finger nails, repeatedly asking for money, when they had run out of finger nails, they smacked her round the head with the same bat rendering her unconscious. They then raided the house turning it upside down taking jewellery, electronics and both their wedding rings. They then left, when the man woke up, he saw his wife unconscious covered in blood and called the police on 999.

This was horrendous and I began rendering first aid whilst I awaited the ambulance to arrive, inside I was screaming, literally what the actual fuck!!! I lost all my grandparents when I was young and this really struck a nerve, how dare somebody enter your home when you are retired, elderly, worked your whole life for some scum bags to come and turn your world upside down.

Daryl McAusland © 2024

Now I was split as part of me wanted to do things right, but the other half of me wanted to find them and torture them. At this point I still hadn't gone that far over and my logical police head won and decided to do things right by the letter of the law.

So, I did my job, I began documenting injuries, house to house enquiries and ensuring the scene was secured for a forensic recovery. I was going to give the detectives the best chance to find these offenders and bring them to justice the right way.

The victims were taken to hospital and the case was handed over to CID to follow up and I was stood down with the comfort it was in hand, that this would be dealt with, it would be dealt with?

Daryl McAusland © 2024

So, the investigation was continued and a vehicle seen close to the scene at the right time was spotted, the report stated there were three occupants in the vehicle.

The DNA came back negative and all other enquiries came back empty, this vehicle was the only lead. Enquiries on the vehicle showed the vehicle having no owner, no insurance, no tax and no MOT. Intelligence on the vehicle linked it to a number of burglaries but no suspects identified. The vehicle was flagged up on police systems for officers to stop to ascertain driver/keeper details.

So, one night I was out on patrol when the vehicle flagged up, I made my way towards where the vehicle was spotted and managed to find it. I pulled the vehicle over and inside were three males, they matched the description of the suspects from the burglary, I took all of their details and then spoke with an officer from CID, I was told to let the vehicle go and they would look into their details.

Daryl McAusland © 2024

So that's what I did, I sent the details to the officer working the case. Surely this would be enough to arrest them? This had to be them and they needed to answer for their crimes.

Nothing was then heard for a few days, so I spoke to the officer in charge who stated he had closed down the case as there was insufficient evidence to proceed. This was not what I wanted to hear, either the officer was lazy or incompetent! But again, people who should be locked away were free to do whatever they pleased.

I was bubbling up inside, like a rage building in my chest, I had their details, it was them! What more did they need? Well, I gave the right way a chance, I tried so hard to not go outside the law but this was too much, something had to be done!

Daryl McAusland © 2024

[CHAPTER 9]

Now this shit was getting real, the justice system failed again so I was being forced to kill 3 more people, this was going to bring my tally up to 5. I was torn as I really wanted to protect the public and do things right but these guys made that really hard! I would have loved to have arrested them and seen them rot in a cell, but this hasn't panned out that way, this had forced my hand and unfortunately if the killing of these people makes you safe in your homes, if it means I can sleep safe at night knowing my family are safe in their beds then it's easy.

Daryl McAusland © 2024

So back to the drawing board, time to plan how I can get all three of these degenerates together and deliver their well-deserved justice.

The more I did this, the more I felt my empathy towards people draining from my soul. The human part of my soul slowly dying, my need to turn to violence easier every time. But this was something I needed to push to the back of my mind, something I needed to forget as I had to plan my next act, my next punishment fitting the crime.

So, I had their details, I knew their addresses and what vehicle they'd be driving.

Now, how do I plan on killing three people and getting away with it?

I had to put together a well organised plan, I checked the activity of the vehicle, whilst out on patrol I'd regularly drive past where the vehicle was parked at the home address. I was then able to establish where they would be, times and everything so I could have access to all three.

Daryl McAusland © 2024

I knew where and when they'd be in the vehicle together so that had to be the place, so it was time to put all my intelligence and planning together to seal their fate.

Time to die, time to pay for your actions, everything was set.

I waited until my rostered days off had started and got to work putting my plan into action.

I got up in the early hours of the morning, got all my gear ready and made my way to where the van was parked. I knew the route the van took every day, so I was able to get everything ready to deal with them.

The three men got into their van as per usual, they drove off along their normal route, down a big hill, now normally the van would start to slow as the driver used the brakes to slow and stop before the junction, however I'd cut their brakes, I was waiting at the bottom of that hill as the van hurtled into a tree at nearly 60mph, knowing what I know from my research they weren't wearing their seatbelts and all three went flying through the windscreen. All three landing pretty much at my feet. They were beaten up, bloodied and struggling to breathe. They were nearly dead, but not quite yet.

I had to have my say before they left this earth. I stood over them making sure their frightened eyes were all on me:

"Gentlemen, you are here today because of your actions, let me remind you, you broke into the home of an elderly couple, you knocked out the husband and tortured the wife by removing her fingernails before knocking her unconscious, I am here today to deliver justice for them and the sentence I impose on you is death"

The men looked up at me, gasping for breath, coughing up blood.

I then picked up a sledgehammer, the look of terror in their eyes, they began pleading but it was an incoherent mess through the blood and broken teeth filling their mouths, they were unable to escape due to their injuries, so almost like a mercy I one by one I smashed them over the head with all my might. Crack, crack, crack all three dead, but made to look like a car crash, blunt force trauma all succumbing to their injuries.

All three lying on the floor, a smashed-up mess, they deserved this! Scum!

I packed up my stuff and quietly made my way home, no trace of my actions.

Weirdly, it was becoming easier to kill, felt like a part of my soul was eroding.

A road traffic accident to cover my tracks, a murder covered up by actions but justice served.

Daryl McAusland © 2024

[CHAPTER 10]

Now everything was quiet for a while, the last murder was put down to a Road Traffic Collison RTC due to vehicle failure, all three were known criminals and the police didn't look too much into it. No harm done; I was still in the clear. The period of nothingness was bliss, no jobs that caused me to blow my top, nothing that allowed the killer in me to surface, I felt free of my demons and was looking forward to the future. I started dating again, going back to the gym and trying really hard to get my life back on track.

I just thought that I had got away with this so far, I wasn't looking over my shoulder constantly and I was happy with what I had achieved. If I wasn't needed to deliver Justice in blood again, I would have been happy with this at peace.

This was all until this...

CAD: 278. UNITS REQUIRED TO REPORTS OF AN ARSON AT LITTLE FARM, VANGUARD WAY, FIRE SERVICE HAVE BEEN CALLED

Now at this point I thought nothing of it, simple arson job, attend do the business and leave. Then back to my life, back to focusing on me. Well, that was the plan and as the old adage says "Man plans and God laughs".

Now I must warn you, this next job was the worst job I had ever been too, because it involved animals, I am an animal lover and humans I can deal with but animals pull at my heart strings. I am the kind of person who can watch films where people get butchered but the minute a dog dies the film goes off.

So, if you can deal with animals being hurt continue, but be warned it's not nice.

So, I turned up to the address, smoke and flames can be seen erupting from a large shed towards the end of the property and the air was filled with smell of burning hair and the loud screams of multiple animals.

What had transpired was that someone had decided that it would be a good idea to burn down a shed full of guinea pigs, small defenceless creatures. Now this angered me more than anything I've ever been too, a human who can do that to defenceless creatures is not fit to be a human, it disgusted me to my stomach and still to this day haunts me.

Daryl McAusland © 2024

I rushed to the shed which was ablaze and was able to pull out the metal crates the guinea pigs were in, this caused a burn to my hand but the adrenaline and the need to save these creatures fuelled me, kept me going, I was not going to let a little pain stop me. The animals were screaming, singed, badly burnt. Some were already dead. I ran the cage to my police car and put them on the back seat. I knew there was a veterinary practice about 10 minutes away so I put on my blue lights and drove at speed, the sound of my sirens drowning out the screams of pain but doing nothing for the smell of burnt hair and flesh.

I was talking to them the whole way, trying to offer them words of support for what it was worth, I felt like I was going to cry, my emotions were high, I was just about keeping it together.

I arrived at the Vets and rushed the cage into the Vetinary practice, the vet took one look at the poor defenceless creatures and said that there was nothing they could do and

Daryl McAusland © 2024

the kindest thing was to euthanise. I then went in with them and stroked them and tried to offer comfort as every single guinea pig that was still alive was given the kindness of the release of death, away from pain.

I was done, I couldn't continue my shift, I had to go home where I cried until it hurt. I eventually passed out due to exhaustion awaking in the night to the smell of those poor defenceless creatures.

This is something that still happens to me now, certain incidents trigger responses in your brain. Certain smells, situations can trigger the emotions to come flooding back, this is what police officers and members of the emergency services have to deal with on a daily basis and then we wonder why the sickness rate is so high? I daren't guess how many first responders have varying degrees of post-traumatic stress disorder PTSD, I know for a fact that I do.

Daryl McAusland © 2024

Now I was mad, I was angry, this was too much and unfortunately for whoever did this I had already decided their fate, once I knew who it was, they were dead.

Daryl McAusland © 2024

[CHAPTER 11]

Now after that I had to take some time, I was not in the right frame of mind and being honest anybody that stepped outside the law at this point was running the risk of being killed for their crimes.

So, a few weeks off, to reset and reevaluate.

I tried to forget what happened, I tried to put it behind me, but the nightmares, the sleepless nights, I don't think I could find peace until they were dealt with.

Back to work, my annual leave finished, ready to put things right. I looked into the crime report regarding the arson and found out that they had a suspect for the job, it was a neighbour dispute, long drawn-out affair that had been going on for ages. The case said that there wasn't enough evidence to proceed, that they had voluntarily interviewed the suspect and the case was closed with no further action. So basically, they were getting away with it and it was making my blood boil, my mind raced as to how best deal with the issue, to deliver real justice.

I was once again torn, the police investigated but the evidence didn't support a conviction, how sure was I that they did it? Could I punish someone without knowing? This really played on my mind, in fact it gave me so much doubt I had to know for myself.

The way I saw it, if I could get my hands on them and ask them questions under some extreme persuasion I'd then know for sure.

So, time to start planning, time to get the truth and then decide how to get justice for those poor animals.

Daryl McAusland © 2024

So, time to add kidnap and torture to my list of crimes, not something I ever saw myself doing but the ends justify the means, right?

Planning stage began, research on who this person was, their habits, routine and possible areas to exploit. I had to ensure that I could get this done without revealing my identity, I was not sure if this was going to end up with me ending their life, so I had to ensure I kept this low key. If they answered my questions correctly and it wasn't them, there was no need to inflict any punishment and they could get on with their lives, however you what happens if they don't pass the test.

Day of reckoning, time to put the wheels in motion, like always I ensured that I was off work so nobody would be looking for me. I rented a van using a fake identity to keep my real name out of it, I made my way to the address and kept myself parked out of sight waiting for them to leave. I waited for a while and just like clockwork they emerged from their house on the way to work. They got into their car and began driving off, I followed at a slight distance, knowing the route they take I had borrowed a police stinger which is a tyre deflating tool, a strip of metal covered in spikes. This was placed across the road, being early in the morning the road wasn't yet used and I had covered it in leaves to conceal it, as we approached, they didn't slow down and then I heard 2 loud bangs as the tyres popped and their brake lights came on. The road was narrow so I stopped behind. They got out of their car and began looking at their tyres, I put on a Covid style face mask pulled up my hood and made my way over offering my help. I said I may have some tools in my van that could be of assistance. They thanked me and began walking to the van, I opened up the side door and ushered them to look inside, as they arrived

Daryl McAusland © 2024

to the side of the van, I had rented they peered inside, this was my time to strike and I smashed him round the back of the head with a crowbar. They slumped forwards into the van unconscious and I pushed the rest of their body inside, I followed them inside closing the door in case anyone was nearby. I handcuffed their hands behind their back and used limb restraints to tie up their legs, finally taping up their mouth with black tape leaving their nose clear to breathe.
I went and collected the stinger and got back into the rear of the van, checked their pulse to make sure they were still alive and then climbed through to the driver's seat from the back.
I had them, time to make my escape and find out the truth, I performed what felt like a hundred-point turn to go the other way.
I had found an abandoned caravan on a farmer's field whilst out on patrol which was perfect.

Daryl McAusland © 2024

I made my way there, checked on sleeping beauty who was still out for the count, now to get them ready. I dragged them inside and tied them to a chair ready for the interrogation. I blacked out all the windows in preparation so inside was pitch black, I splashed them with water to wake them up and shone a bright torch in their face. They awoke with a start, eyes darting around with a look of panic and fear.

I said to them: -

"I'm going to ask you yes, no questions. You are gagged so I want you to respond with your head, do you understand?"

They nodded in agreement, still looking terrified.

"If you want any chance of walking out of here alive, I want the truth, answer truthfully or I will kill you, do you understand?"

Again, a quick frantic nod for yes.

"Ok, did you set fire to your neighbours shed?"

Nothing, just staring into the torchlight.

"Answer the question"

Again nothing, so obviously he needed some persuasion, I put a tea towel over his face pushed his head back and began pouring water over his face, I had seen this in a movie and it actually worked as they began snorting water as they were being drowned through their nostrils.

I stopped, took off the towel, let them catch their breath and asked again:

"Did you burn down that shed? Answer or you get more"

The initial water boarding seemed to have worked as they hesitantly nodded for yes. I had enough and I know I said they would have a chance of leaving alive, but only if they were innocent and I knew differently.

"Ok, thank you for your honesty, I am just going to get something to cut you free"

I left the caravan, I also lied as I shut the door and began covering the caravan in petrol, he was going to be given the same treatment, eye for an eye. I lit the fuel with a lighter and got into the van, watching the caravan become engulfed in flames, he must have been going crazy inside as it was rocking from side to side as the flames intensified. Time to go, dead or soon to be it was done. All evidence of me burned in the caravan. I drove away with the sight of the caravan windows blowing out in my wing mirror as it was fully ablaze.

I dropped off the van and left the keys in the letterbox for returns.

I was done, I was hoping that they weren't responsible for killing those animals to try and end my killing spree but humanity never fails to disappoint and justice again was served.

I was beginning to dislike the person I was becoming, killing for the greater good was paying an awful toll on my own humanity and health.

Daryl McAusland © 2024

I again started making myself empty promises to stop, last one, never again. Even started praying asking for forgiveness and making promises to stop in exchange for salvation, my sanity was starting to slip.

I believe deep in my soul that I am a good man, but this thirst for blood was consuming me, my twisted views on justice, ethics and morality were blurring the lines of what is considered good and bad, was I becoming evil? Was I too far gone?

Daryl McAusland © 2024

[CHAPTER 12]

Slight update on my life at this point, I had killed 6 people so far, if you had been paying attention I was convicted of 10.

At this point in my life, I felt like I was invincible, that I was too clever to be caught but the toll it had taken on my mental health and my humanity was high.

I was suffering from recurring nightmares of the things I had done and the fear of being caught was playing havoc with my anxiety.

The lack of sleep was making me unwell and due to this was having a detrimental effect on my sickness record and I was close to being reported at work under their absence policy. My supervisor had noticed a change in my demeanour and complaints around incivility and use of force to the public were starting to get attention and to top it all off I was being referred to occupational health as they were concerned.

So, to put it bluntly at this point in my life I was drowning and could feel that I was losing touch with myself.

Onwards and upwards, I still had a job to do and bills to pay, I was trying my hardest to steer clear of incidents that would attract my attention, almost like a Jeckle and Hyde situation with the murderous part of my personality dormant unless awoken by injustice, almost like I was trying to bury him down to the back of my mind so he couldn't surface.

But life is never that easy and this happened...

CAD: 204. UNITS TO ATTEND 56 PARSONAGE CRESCENT, FEMALE AT THE ADDRESS HAS MADE ALLEGATIONS OF A SEXUAL ASSAULT THAT OCCURRED IN A TAXI ON HER WAY HOME, SEXUAL OFFENCE TRAINED OFFICER TO BE DEPLOYED

Being trained as a specialist officer I was deployed and made my way to the address.

Upon arrival I was met by a young girl in her late teens, she had been out on a night out with her friends and got a taxi home, on the way home the taxi driver pulled over and got into the back with the girl and started touching the girl in a sexual way, groping her and trying to kiss her, she froze and eventually asked to go home, the taxi driver then got back into the driver's seat and took her home. The girl got into the address and broke down to her parents crying and police were called. This girl was devastated and crying as she had been through a traumatic ordeal, she was scared of the man coming back as he knew where she lived and to rub salt into the wounds she had to pay for the privilege. So, I decided this one I would see through, I would deal with all of it, I would take the statements, obtain the evidence, arrest the suspect and then present my case to the crown prosecution service.

I decided I would give the law one more chance, one more time to show me that there was another way, another way to get justice.

So that's what I did, I took hours writing the best statement I've ever taken, I obtained all the evidence, I went to the taxi office located the suspect and arrested him, I took him into interview and put the allegations to him. He partially admitted to what he had done but stated that it was a cultural discrepancy, he was doing something in his culture and it was a misunderstanding.

Daryl McAusland © 2024

BULLSHIT!!! I did not believe a word, but I had enough evidence to go for an early charge decision with the Crown prosecution service, this is what I did, hours on the phone waiting to eventually get through to a lawyer who decided to side with the suspect, I argued and was told that they wanted to discontinue the case and release with no charge. I really really wanted this to be the one case that showed me the light, so I didn't give up, I was so confident in the evidence, that it proved his guilt even if it was her word against his. So, I escalated it, I went to my Inspector and made my case, they agreed and they went back to the crown prosecution service to challenge the decision. I thought finally we would get justice, finally trusting the system was the way forward, No!

They came back with the same outcome; he was free to go and with him leaving went my faith in the justice system.

Daryl McAusland © 2024

So, he was released, free to go, but not for long, I was coming for him!

Daryl McAusland © 2024

[CHAPTER 13]

Here we go again, problem is now I had lost all respect for the justice system. That one last chance I gave it to prove it wasn't broken, it wasn't biased towards the criminals, that even when I had a water tight case it still went to shit. So now I was really done, I had now become judge, jury and executioner.

That part of me that joined the police with visions of doing things the right way, the upstanding member of community, the squeaky-clean police officer was dead.

So, this taxi driver was going to be an easy fix, I'd started to not care about getting caught and if I was honest, I welcomed it, I had snowballed into this monster who just wanted blood and I wasn't happy with what I'd become, but the murderous part of my personality had taken over and was now dominating my personality, it was now near impossible to suppress. I had evolved into what I hated but nothing was going to stop me from achieving justice.

The planning was easy, I just had to book a taxi in a fake name to be picked up from a remote location, I asked the taxi office for the driver by name and it was all set.

So, I got prepared, I wasn't trying to hide my identity, I was going to let this bastard know who I was before getting the justice required. I went to the location at the set time as planned and waited, shortly after arriving I saw the headlights of a car slowly approaching, I could see faintly in the dark it was the same taxi driver from the incident, he pulled over opened his window and asked if I was waiting for a taxi. He didn't seem to recognise me and I nodded, the car unlocked and I got in the car sitting behind him. The usual small talk began as we drove off, I had given a remote end destination for the final act. As we drove, the car eventually became silent as the small talk dried up leaving me to my thoughts. I was having a battle in my head between good and bad, weighing up reasons to let him live and reasons to kill him, the constant thoughts of what he did interrupting my debate causing my anger to rise, flashbacks of the girl crying, flashbacks of my mother crying, everything bad that had happened in my life was muddling together and my rage was growing, I was still deep in debate as the car stopped and we had arrived. I was asked if this was the place and before he could ask any more questions I had reached over his head from behind and had cheese wire pressed against his throat pulling backwards so that he was pinned back against the seat, he began pleading telling me to take the money, his voice was panicked and scared.

Daryl McAusland © 2024

"DO YOU THINK I WANT YOUR MONEY!! YOU FUCKING DISGUST ME"

I was angry and shouted at him, the cheek of it thinking I was some simple robber, how fucking dare he!

I pulled the wire tighter and a bead of blood started running down his neck, he began to struggle so I pulled tighter:

"YOU SEXUALLY ABUSED A YOUNG GIRL AND THOUGHT YOU GOT AWAY WITH IT, YOU FUCKING DIDNT"

He was thrashing his arms and legs screaming for help, I pulled the wire even tighter getting ready to tell him his fate but the moment I pulled that wire there was a large gush of blood which erupted from his throat all over the windscreen. In my rage I had pulled too tight and had severed his main artery, shit! Blood was pumping out like a water fountain and he was dead! I didn't even get to give him his sentence and now the car was covered in blood.

Daryl McAusland © 2024

The blood came out so violently it hit the windscreen and splashed back hitting me in the face and I was covered. Shit! Ok time to get the fuck out of here!

My rage had caused my normal careful planning to go to shit! I was covered in his DNA, I needed to get rid of all my clothes and have a shower but I hadn't planned for this. It had been raining during the day so there were puddles and I was able to wash my hands and face in the dirty water.

I had to leave the car there, the body there and everything there, this was a mess, a fucking mess!! I didn't prepare for this and now I was at a loose end.

I had to get home across the countryside to ensure I wasn't seen using the cover of darkness. I needed to get a handle on my anger as losing myself like that had really put me in a bad position, the plan was to have used the car to get away closer to my address and then burn the car with him inside, but as I had covered myself, the windscreen and the

Daryl McAusland © 2024

whole front of the car in blood and had a semi- decapitated corpse in the front seat, I panicked and fled.

This could be bad, I potentially left my DNA and evidence in the back of the car, being a taxi meant there would be multiple traces of DNA but still a chance I could get looked at and this wasn't good.

Living my life with the fear of being arrested around the corner plaguing me was not what I had envisioned.

Daryl McAusland © 2024

[CHAPTER 14]

So having to live with the fear of being arrested looking over my shoulder was not great for my health, my sleep was worse than ever and my anxiety was causing me not to eat, I was starting to look dishevelled and gaunt.

My external appearance was starting to match my soul, sick and broken.

My tolerance for people was little to none and I feared for the safety of anyone that broke the law bad enough to warrant being punished under my own personal justice system.

I was still at work, just! The complaints were circling and I was under investigation for multiple things due to my disdain for the public, my life was a mess, but I still felt like I was doing the right thing, I was the innocents saviour and I was developing a hero complex. I felt my actions were just and true like the comics you read as a child.

To make matters worse, the car was found with the body inside, it was big news! All over the papers, tv and social media. This was also being investigated by the big guns, the (MIT) major investigation team, they deal with all the most serious, high-profile cases and they are good! Very good to the point that it was making me nervous, but until I see them vultures circling coming for me, I was just going to push that to the back of my mind and carry on until that day comes.

Daryl McAusland © 2024

So normal day, normal shit, dealing with the daily bullshit that is modern day policing. Shoplifting, thefts, public order just general rubbish that people couldn't sort out themselves and needed a police officer to sort out their lives. I was on route to such a call, reports had come in of a female who had been detained for stealing cosmetics, bog standard job, didn't take too much brain power, caught on CCTV, stopped by security and just needed me to arrest and process, like I said easy routine shit!

How fucking wrong could I be, I turned up unaware of what events were about to happen that would potentially ruin my life forever.

So, I pulled up at the shop and made my way inside, nonchalant, I was bored and just going through the motions. Probably links in to why what happened, happened.

Daryl McAusland © 2024

I was ushered to a security room by staff and they opened the door, inside was a female, sat down at a table, without sounding like I was stereotyping but she looked like a junkie, she was dirty, messy hair, ripped unwashed clothes, no shoes and her feet were black.

The security guard told me what had happened, he stated that she was seen on CCTV hiding packets of meat under her clothing. I asked the female if she had heard the allegation and she grunted. I then instructed the female that she was under arrest and to stand up so I could handcuff her for my safety and to transport her to a custody facility. She stood up and before I had a chance to do anything she spat what looked like blood into my face, it hit me just below the nose and went into my mouth. She then began laughing hysterically and told me she had HIV. Oh fuck, I was pissed!! I punched her so hard in her face she was knocked unconscious. I then handcuffed her and asked for more units to assist. If I was in that room on my own without cameras, she would be dead, I only allowed her to live to save my own skin, don't get me wrong she would be dead, but later! I didn't realise what I was about to go through and the hell my life was about to become.

Due to her being unconscious an ambulance was called and, on their arrival, I informed them what had happened and I was taken to hospital as well, fuck my life!!turns out this was a credible threat to my ongoing life, that I had a real possibility of contracting HIV, that this action could possibly end my life.

To say I was shitting myself would have been an understatement.

I'm man enough to admit for the first time in my adult life I was truly scared and terrified, this was my worst fear realised.

The female suspect was taken over by other officers and I was now in the hands of our NHS, the amazing army of

Daryl McAusland © 2024

doctors and nurses who were there to do everything they could to make sure I was ok.

I was seen by a doctor who immediately administered me with a post-exposure prophylaxis which is a drug administered after exposure in emergencies to prevent HIV. I was then informed I had to take HIV medication every day for the next 28 days and that the side effects were going to be brutal, but if I lasted the course that at the end the chances of having contracted HIV would be greatly reduced. Then once I'd finished the month of hell, I would be given a blood test and then and only then would I be able to know if I was in the clear.

Fuck me, this was going to be a month from hell!!!

Daryl McAusland © 2024

[CHAPTER 15]

Home from the hospital and I felt like shit, my head was pounding, my stomach was churning, feeling like I was going to vomit and the world around me was spinning.

I had a gruelling month ahead of me, but the thought of killing that worthless excuse of a human being was all that I could think about.
How dare she, how fucking dare she!
In my mind I was a hero, I was out there in the mud fighting the injustice of the world and she had the audacity to spit in my face and not only that, blood infected with HIV.

Daryl McAusland © 2024

Oh, I was livid and I was struggling to find a way to inflict the punishment that fit the crime.

This was something I had a long time to plot and fester over.

So, 28 days, 28 doses of medication, 28 days of horrible side effects.

The side effects being loss of appetite, headache, difficulty in sleeping, abnormal dreams, depression, dizziness, vertigo, abdominal pain, bloating, flatulence, diarrhoea, nausea, vomiting, indigestion, rash, weakness, fatigue and fever.

So, I had a mix of these symptoms every single day, nonstop for a month, I didn't leave my bed, I hardly ate and lost a whole month of my life. The worst part was having the fear of having HIV dangling over my head. Add the extra pressure of my slowly declining mental health and I was in a real bad way.

Daryl McAusland © 2024

So, to say I was angry was an understatement, my every waking thought was how to exact my revenge!

The 28 days passed and I was still alive, just! I had to go back to the hospital and have a blood test to see if I was in the clear. Luckily for me it did, I was a walking skeleton, I had the appearance of a vagrant with long unkempt hair and beard but all was worth it knowing that I didn't have HIV.

I was happy, but I still didn't forget who had put me through this, who had put my life through living hell.

I still couldn't go back to work, I had to go and see occupational health, I had to put on weight, clean myself up and then I could get to delivering justice.

Daryl McAusland © 2024

So, all in all nearly 2 months off work, but I was back, fresh and had a new sense of purpose. Time to get shit done.

I researched the case and found out that she had been charged by the police and was currently on bail awaiting a court date, now the old me, the version who used to believe in the justice system would have let this happened, but there was no way on earth I was going to allow her to wriggle her way out of this. Besides there was no punishment the courts could inflict that would be comparable to the damage she had done to me; this was personal and I was going to get my justice.

Daryl McAusland © 2024

[CHAPTER 16]

Back where I belong, I was welcomed back to work in the traditional way, with cakes at the work's briefing, now if you aren't aware of police traditions if you make a mistake, it's your birthday or just because your told, you have to buy cakes for your entire team. So, I sat in briefing watching my team stuff their faces with cakes I'd bought, the fine was for me nearly dying, it's weird, I know.

I was back, so this gave me back my access to the police systems, which meant I could start plotting her demise.

Daryl McAusland © 2024

The vultures not yet circling for my job, but the constant reminder that I had changed as my sickness record and work record were both shown as unacceptable and with Performance review pending, I knew I was going to be getting a hefty kick up the arse and the possibility of sanctions which lead onto that slippery slope of dismissal.

I may now come across as a heartless, murdering monster with no empathy, no compassion and a strong persuasion to extreme violence. However, I still loved what the police stood for, how you can choose to live your life helping others, I had unfortunately gone outside of the rules and knew one slip up was enough to end it all, anyway I was in my eyes a hero, a modern-day Robin Hood.

Now back to getting my own justice!!

Daryl McAusland © 2024

I was able to determine everything I needed to know about her so I could do what was required and a plan was made. After the last fiasco I was extra diligent in planning this as I wasn't going to run the risk of coming short again or losing my temper and putting myself at risk of being caught.

So, I finished work, as I had been away for so long, I was allowed to spend the whole day doing administrative work, so between my emails, crime complaints and general queries I had built up my master plan. Having unlimited access to the police station I was able to get everything I needed and got changed and left, but I wasn't going home, I was going to make things right.

I had found out through intelligence that she would regularly go to a certain location to buy her drugs, now knowing this I had laced my own white powder with a very strong sedative. I arrived in the area earlier than the reports

Daryl McAusland © 2024

indicated she would be there, I found her drug dealer and a mix of not getting arrested and a healthy donation to his funds meant he was willing to sell her my special mix, no questions asked. I took myself off and watched from a distance out of view.

Then she arrived, the disgusting creature looking very similar in appearance and dress as before came staggering down the road, she approached my new friend the drug dealer and an exchange was made. Now old me would have been arresting both for their involvement but my interests laid elsewhere and I was willing to overlook the crime. She then left and I followed from a distance, she then turned into an alleyway and I hurried to catch up just getting a glimpse of her going to sit down behind a large bin, obviously this was where she would be taking her drugs and so I waited, I was watching the bin for a good 20 minutes before I decided to investigate further, surely enough time lapsed. I carefully walked up to the bin and down beside the bin she was sprawled out unconscious, she was alive but completely out of it. I gave her a few kicks for good measure to ensure she was away with fairies. I could have killed her there, but this wasn't what I had planned for her, you don't get to ruin my life and then peacefully leave this world. She had to know it was me and she didn't deserve the kindness of a nice way out!

Step 1 complete, now onto stage 2, I went and got my car, pulled up to the bin and put her in the boot and then drove off, successfully I had got her and I was so pleased with myself, happy and smiling. A stark contrast to when I began this journey.

So, I had decided that as she had completely torn my life apart, she should get a similar treatment, an act that will completely have her in bits, literally.

Daryl McAusland © 2024

So, I drove to a bridge, not just any bridge, a remote bridge that goes over train tracks, the tracks service high speed trains that are not going slow, hundreds of tons of metal travelling nearly 100mph.

I opened the boot and she was still out for the count, no internal conversation with myself telling me to stop, both parts of my brain chanting kill, kill, kill.

I picked her up, she wasn't very heavy, but being addicted to class A drugs does that to you. I walked over to the bridge and roused her, she opened her eyes slowly still groggy from the drugs and looked at me, she knew instantly who I was and said questioning "You?"

I looked at her and said "goodbye" and then threw her off the bridge onto the tracks below, she landed with a large thud and what sounded like cracks, I believe I had broken her legs as when I looked down, she was trying to scramble off the tracks with just one arm.

Daryl McAusland © 2024

A loud horn could be heard, the vibrations of a train shaking the tracks and the bridge, then in the distance the headlights of a train, moving very very fast. She began screaming still trying to scramble out of the way, I heard the loud screech of brakes and the horn being sounded repeatedly. Large trains at speed take forever to stop due to the weight of the locomotive, so I wasn't scared it was actually going to stop, I looked down she was right there in its path and then, well being honest I looked away, even I had some aversion to gore. The train eventually stopped and I left in a hurry, I knew the deed was done and I had got my own personal justice.

I wasn't overly worried about getting caught as she was a drug user and I didn't think anyone would really care, also being on the tracks made it look like a suicide, death by train is sadly more prevalent than you think and the statistics are a sad reflection of our failings dealing with people in crisis in the United Kingdom.

It felt like a weight had been lifted, I was a new man. She took a month of my life and she got what she deserved.

Back to normal, back to being me, I was determined to sort myself out, I had made peace with myself and knew that I had changed so much, just had to live with my new persona, the more I killed the more I changed, like a metamorphosis.

Daryl McAusland © 2024

[CHAPTER 17]

CAD: 378. MULTIPLE 999 CALLS FROM MEMBERS OF THE PUBLIC. REPORTS OF A SMALL HATCHBACK CAR DRIVING DOWN THE MOTORWAY THE WRONG DIRECTION INTO ONCOMING TRAFFIC, FIRE AND AMBULANCE ON STANDBY, UNITS TO ASSIST

Guess where I was going? So, I was driving around on patrol as you do, looking for anything suspicious, anything that I could get my teeth into and investigate, looking for that career making stop that would elevate my career when the radio sparked into action and we were asked to assist with this job, now I was the closest unit, double crewed and I made my way. On route discussing with my colleague that if we saw the vehicle coming towards us on the motorway that we would have to put ourselves in harm's way to stop them, that the vehicle couldn't be allowed to go past us. We both agreed and sat in silence, I was deep in thought with the possibility of crashing into a car head on, the potential risk I was putting myself in, however as a police officer it is your job to save life and limb as your main directive, even so I was shitting myself as the thought of dying wasn't really on my agenda, well not yet.

This silence was quickly broken as a further call over the radio came in saying that the vehicle had struck another vehicle in the outside lane at over 70mph and for units to assist urgently, this was not far from where I was travelling so I called up and increased my speed to get to the scene.

Daryl McAusland © 2024

Upon arrival it was total carnage there was a small car smashed to bits, all parts of it covering the road and there was a large German 4x4 with its front wheel missing, front drivers side bumper completely caved in. The traffic was all stationary behind and so I positioned my car to make sure it was a safe place to work and then my colleague ran to the 4x4 and I made my way to the small car. Inside the car were 2 men, the driver was in a bad way, gasping for breath and asking for help, the passenger was silent, now when triaging patients, you always go to the quiet ones first as the noisy ones are alive. I got into the passenger side and began asking if the passenger could hear me, he was sat head fully back against the headrest looking up. I placed my fingers on his neck to check for a pulse, any signs of life. With this the man's face fell forwards unattached from his body leaving a large gaping hole where it should be. Quite honestly the most horrific thing I have ever seen, the man was dead. Upon impact the engine bulk head had been

Daryl McAusland © 2024

pushed forward into the cars cabin towards the passenger and the passenger had been thrown forwards towards the bulkhead, they met and it completely sliced through his face chin to top of head, as the car stopped, he was thrown backwards and his face was resting on his body until I checked for an airway and pulse and caused his body to fall forwards. It was like a scene out of a horror movie and I was not impressed, the driver seeing the passengers head fall off began crying and sobbing uncontrollably.

Now an investigation would normally be conducted, the driver would go to hospital, be arrested for death by dangerous driving, court, prison etc but no, this was being dealt with right now, I was on my own with him whilst my colleague assisted with the other car.

I made my way round to the driver's side, he stunk of alcohol and I was fuming, I hadn't yet processed what I had seen so my only reaction was one of pure hatred.

Daryl McAusland © 2024

I got into his side which hadn't taken as much impact and told him I was going to check for any injuries and to render first aid.

I put my hands on his neck and said I was checking for a pulse and then proceeded to strangle the man, I gripped his throat so tightly and whispered:

"THIS IS WHAT YOU GET, YOU KILLED YOUR FRIEND SO IM KILLING YOU"

I could feel the pulse in his neck racing and starting to slow the harder I squeezed, his eyes bulging out of his head and his breathing becoming laboured. Due to the crash, he was weak and was struggling to fight back, his arms flailing to no avail and quite quickly he was dead.

The bastard got exactly what he deserved!

I could see more blue lights approaching, ambulance and other police cars, I updated the radio that the vehicle responsible for the crash had 2 male occupants, both men were dead on police arrival.

Daryl McAusland © 2024

I then looked back into the car, the passenger's headless body and the driver dead staring into emptiness, I was violently sick, the smells, the sight everything became too much as the adrenaline started to fade. I felt out of control and that I was having a panic attack, I had to get myself together, I needed to make sure that this was believable. I was met by other officers and paramedics who got into the vehicle pronouncing them dead, they looked over both bodies and were happy that the injuries sustained and their deaths were due to the car crash, once again I had got away with it and had their rubber stamp to hide my crime, but still I had got the passenger justice as the driver, his friend had acted in a way that cost him his life.

A weight lifted, another sigh of relief, I didn't know how many more times I could dodge getting caught, but at this point I was still in the clear.

Daryl McAusland © 2024

Now the driver of the 4x4, the innocent party seemed to have a guardian angel, as he was able to get out of his car, walk around injury free, his car had lost a wheel and significant front damage, but he was absolutely fine, a true miracle. Also pays credit to German engineering as the 2 vehicles couldn't be further apart with their damage and the fates of their occupants.

Due to the emotional and mental stress the incident potentially could have put on me I was allowed to go home, this used to be somewhere I could relax and take solitude but more and more began to feel like a prison where the ghosts of my past visited me over and over in my head, reliving my mistakes and the thought of being caught stopping me from sleeping.

At this point in my life I had turned to good old-fashioned alcohol, every night downing a bottle of high percentage spirits to knock me into a stupor, not real sleep but enough to keep me going.

I was spiralling as my tolerance to alcohol was getting more, so I needed to drink more to knock me out, a vicious cycle pushing me to my body's limits.

[CHAPTER 18]

So, everything in my life was falling apart, I couldn't hold down a relationship, I was drowning in debt, my alcoholism was having negative effects on my body and I was convinced I was starting to go a shade of yellow due to my liver not being happy with its daily pickling.

I know I sound like a real catch!

Now this was where my life had got to, this was the moment for me just before disaster, I was either going to get caught, die from the abuse I was putting my body through or get sacked as I had deviated so far away from my original purpose, to uphold the law and help people. I was intolerant of people, convinced that I was their saviour and they should be thankful to me, I didn't feel like they were deserving of my civility and so the risk of being shown the door was an ever-increasing threat.

But this is what actually happened, this was why it all came to an end, you will notice from my charge sheet that there were 10 murders I was found guilty of, well this is number 10, the last one and why I got caught.

CAD: 410. 999 CALL, POLICE REQUIRED TO ATTEND 65 THE CLOSE, FEMALE AT ADDRESS HAS FLED THERE AFTER A VIOLENT DOMESTIC, FEMALE ON SCENE WITH INJURIES, AMBULANCE HAS BEEN CALLED.

Daryl McAusland © 2024

Not knowing what fate was about to greet me I made my way to the address, now domestic incidents have always been my least favourite thing to attend, they always bring back painful memories and I can't help but think about my mother every single time, now this mixed in with my new found hero complex was not a good mix as I would have given anything to be able to go back in time and save my mother from the abuse she received.

I turned up to the address and was initially greeted by the homeowner who told me to come inside where the victim was, upon entering the room I was met with the sight of a woman roughly my age with a black eye and an egg sized lump protruding from her eyebrow, her mascara was running and she was trying to talk but kept crying and having to stop to catch her breath. It transpired she had been in a long-term violent relationship with her partner who regularly would get drunk and then beat the absolute shit out of her, the only reason she fled tonight was that it didn't stop and he had been trying to strangle her and she feared for her life. This was a regular occurrence where she would report the incident to police, we would take action, she would then drop the charges and claim it was fabricated and he was innocent, this unfortunately is very common in these types of incidents and why most murders are domestic related, the abuse gets worse, the offender keeps getting away with it until one day they push it too far and then death!

My blood was boiling, I felt like a comic book character with steam escaping from my ears, I was not happy that this man felt it was acceptable to do this, to regularly assault his partner and for there to be no punishment, well he needed to be dealt with, as I was with other colleagues it was best that we went and arrested him. Any later punishment could be delivered afterwards. So, we got the address and off we went. Upon arrival we knocked on the door and there was no answer, I checked on the driveway his car was still present, I could see a downstairs window was ajar, I opened the window and called inside for the man to present himself, nothing.

The room was a bedroom with a double bed in the middle of the room, I had the mobile phone number of the suspect and called the phone, I could hear it ringing from the other side of the bed that I couldn't see. I called up on the radio for more units to attend and then my colleague climbed in through the window announcing it was the police. As soon as he was in the room a man jumped up from behind the bed and ran at my colleague punching him violently to the face, my colleague went down and it looked as if he was unconscious.

Now I saw red, I was in a rage and I jumped through the window, rugby tackled the man to the floor and began punching him to the face, left, right, left, right repeatedly.

Daryl McAusland © 2024

I was like an animal, all I could see was the face of my father who had abused my mother, I was getting my own back.

I stopped punching to catch my breath and the man was bloodied, his nose was broken, his eyes were partially closed and he was still breathing, just.

I was so angry and couldn't stop myself, I had decided there and then that I was going to kill him, he would be punished for what he had done and so I took both my thumbs and pressed them into his eyes, grabbing the back of his head and I began to squeeze like I was trying to make his head pop, he was screaming, arms legs kicking out, trying to free himself.

I could feel his eyes squishing under my thumbs, blood pouring out of his eye sockets. Whilst doing this I was screaming "Die, Die, Die!!!"

Whilst this was going on I heard other police officers coming in through the window, they grabbed hold of me

Daryl McAusland © 2024

and were trying to get me off, I had lost it and they weren't going to stop me, I was being shouted at and grabbed but I held on and squeezed as hard as I could and then there was a sudden smack to the back of my head and everything went dark.

Turned out one of the officers took out his baton and struck me around the head causing me to lose consciousness, the only saving grace in my opinion was that they were too late as he was already dead before they could stop me, another person taken off the streets who were a danger to women, I saved everyone from him.

So, the next thing I remember was having the worst headache of my life, not yet opening my eyes but the sound of an electronic heart beat monitor beeping away, I slowly opened my eyes adjusting my eyes to the light, fuck my head hurt, I felt sick. I tried to move my arms to wipe the sleep from out of my eyes but couldn't, I was handcuffed to

Daryl McAusland © 2024

a hospital bed. I've looked around still slightly squinting to see a police officer sat in a chair in the room.

Ok, would appear I'm fucked!

[CHAPTER 19]

I had been arrested for the murdering the pathetic excuse of a man from that last job, they still hadn't worked out that I was responsible for more.

Horrible feeling, having everything stripped from you, my warrant card was gone and with it my sense of identity.

The hospital gave me the all clear, no concussion and nothing broken so I was free to be transported to a police custody facility and then put into a cell. I didn't deserve this, that man, in-fact everyone that I had killed deserved it!

Daryl McAusland © 2024

I should be getting some medal of valour not thrown away into a cell.

This was very surreal being on the other side of the desk, being looked at like a criminal, hunter turned prey, was not something I overly enjoyed and being honest I felt humiliated as I didn't belong here.

But that's where I ended up, in a tiny cell with a metal toilet and a blue mattress bed, nothing else with the added privilege of a camera watching me 24/7.

This was where I was to remain until I had my police interview.

Now I was torn, I could try and fabricate a story to get off, try and trick my way out of this conundrum. But by this point I was too far gone; I honestly didn't think I had done anything wrong and that taking his life was necessary.

So, the minutes turned into hours of sitting there waiting, the thoughts of my life haunting me, the early years of my

Daryl McAusland © 2024

mother, the recent cases I'd delivered my own justice. The thoughts of the victims and the justice I got for them providing me with a sense of accomplishment and comfort, I had decided that I wasn't going to hide my deeds but I wasn't pleading guilty! I was going to make my case that I did what they feared, what they wouldn't and at the end of the day I believed if they were brave enough, they would have done the same thing.

I was offered a solicitor to represent me before interview, I was so convinced that I was in the right that I didn't think I would need one, there was nothing they could say that would dissuade me from, I wanted everyone to know my story and why I did what I did, I understand not everyone agrees with my course of action but let's be honest you can't judge me, nobody can and I answered to nobody.

Daryl McAusland © 2024

So, into interview I went, it was me on one side and 2 experienced detectives on the other, they went through all the legal parts first and then into the interview we went with their opening gambit do you know why you are here today?

Well, I didn't hold back:

"Well, you are here to interview me about the man I killed last night, but I would also like to talk to you about the fact that he was my tenth and I don't consider them murders, I consider them justice killings due to the failings of the legal system, you should be thanking me."

The look of shock on the detectives faces, a slight pause and then they asked me about the rest, for the next 2 hours I gave them every single detail of everything I had done and why, I also told them that I wasn't guilty of any crime. The interview ended and I was eventually charged and remanded in custody until my court appearance, you already know what happened at court, ridiculous!

Daryl McAusland © 2024

Now you may be wondering why would I own up to everything? Why would I help them knowing I probably could have got away with the rest? Well, the answer is that I wanted them to know, I wanted to let the world know, if you don't deal with the bad people in society then people like me will. That there are heroes among us who will tread where others dare not and let's be honest, I don't actually think I done anything wrong. You may disagree but how many people have I saved from being brutally attacked, robbed, sexually assaulted? Did my actions outweigh the good I did? Well unfortunately that is something we will never know; however, I am content in myself I have done the right thing.

Issue I now face, is that old saying "If you can't do the time, don't do the crime"

Daryl McAusland © 2024

[CHAPTER 20]

So, now you know everything, you can make your mind up if what I did was right, if my actions were justified, if my soul can be redeemed.

I started out on this journey to do the right thing, to protect the most vulnerable in society from the most dangerous. I feel that my actions were proportionate considering the lack of support the police receive in the conviction of offenders. Now I am not in any way having a go at the police, the crown prosecution service or the court systems as they are in place to deal with offenders and the police and emergency services put themselves in harm's way on a regular basis. I feel that the systems in place needs to be

Daryl McAusland © 2024

reviewed, needs to be made more victim focused, dealing with the offenders robustly in a way that doesn't make someone like me question everything, decide that taking the law into their hands was the only option.

The question you may have, do I regret my actions? Unequivocally No! Every single person that received their justice, their punishment in my mind deserved it. If the courts won't lock them up then I will make sure they can't do no more harm.

As I have said before, my actions now may make me a criminal, a murderer, a vigilante but history will be my true judge and I will hopefully be remembered as a hero, someone willing to stand up for the weak.

End of the day, the only person who can really judge us is God, at our end when we are held accountable for our actions, will I be deemed good or bad? Or will I be welcomed much like the Archangel Michael for killing in the name of God?

Daryl McAusland © 2024

Nobody knows what awaits us at the end, is this is it? Do we cease to exist, that's it, nothing, just a black empty void of nothing. Does everything we do throughout our lives, learning, growing and bettering ourselves mean nothing? Or is it the case that there is a god, there is a greater being that made us, gave us purpose and everything that happened is for a grand purpose?

Well, these are all questions that everyone has, some believe in the afterlife without any doubt and some have their doubts.
The only way to truly know is to face that final adventure and to die.

So, everything I have told you, from beginning to end has been my final confession, I am an ex-police officer and we don't fare well in prison. I would rather leave this earth on my terms than at the hands of some criminal.

Daryl McAusland © 2024

So, my final thoughts before the end, I have lived my life to the best of abilities, ensuring that I have put the needs of people in need before my own. I only hope that my parents understand why I did what I did, why letting bad people remain was not an option and the only thing I regret is letting my soul be tarnished by my actions.

I wrote a poem whilst sat in prison pondering my fate, I shall leave it with you as my last act before the end

"Deaths warm embrace, beckoning, calling me to a place of no pain
If you've never felt loss, heartbreak or depression it's hard to explain
No feeling, a numb vacant heart, the shadows drawing in
A life plans gone, purpose vacated, reliving past mistakes, where do I begin

Daryl McAusland © 2024

To the outside looking in, I seem happy without a care

A mask I wear, a role I play, on my own I am lost, alone, nowhere

Trying to find purpose, peace, a new direction to head

Ignoring the demons, facing the truth, a solitary path to tread

The constant overwhelming urge to fade, disappear, evaporate into sorrow

Clinging on to hope, the future and a better tomorrow"

So that's it, PC Jack Morgan signing off.

THE END

Daryl McAusland © 2024